William Shakespeare's

Julius Caesar

EDITED BY
Christina Lacie

ILLUSTRATED BY
Michele Earle-Bridges

BARRON'S

All inquiries should be addressed to:
Barron's Educational Series, Inc.
250 Wireless Boulevard
Hauppauge, New York 11788
www.barronseduc.com

ISBN-13: 978-0-7641-3279-7
ISBN-10: 0-7641-3279-2

Library of Congress Control No.: 2005930773

Printed in China
9 8 7 6 5 4 3 2 1

Contents

About the play

The Tragedy of Julius Caesar, or *Julius Caesar,* as it is commonly known, is a tragedy as its proper name implies. A tragedy is a serious dramatic work in which the audience (or, in this case, the reader) witnesses the downfall of the main character, otherwise known as the protagonist. The reasons behind the main character's downfall are varied. In most of Shakespeare's tragedies, however, the main character usually dies in the final act, which is Act V. But *Julius Caesar* is different. The title character dies in the third act and two other prominent characters (Cassius and Brutus) follow in Act V—proving the downfall of major characters in a tragedy.

This play is about a famous, ancient Roman general and leader named Julius Caesar, who actually was a real person. Upon returning from several years of fighting to gain more territory for Rome, he is chosen to be the dictator. Originally, he was one of three men who ruled Rome; they were called a Triumvirate. However, Caesar began a civil war and ended up murdering one of the two other Triumvirs—a man named Pompey. Caesar was then accused of being power hungry, and it was this desire for power, coupled with an arrogant personality, that initiated the jealousy and anger in Cassius and Brutus. The two men plot to kill Caesar with the assistance of many other Roman nobles, who agree with their perspectives on Caesar. This wicked plot to assassinate Caesar, however, returns to haunt Cassius and Brutus; they both die by committing suicide.

Shakespeare took liberty in condensing three years of action into three days. *Julius Caesar* might be one of Shakespeare's shorter tragedies, but it is also far less complicated than the others—making it a play that is much easier to understand.

Literary terms

alliteration The repetition of one or more beginning sounds, usually consonants, in a group of words.

allusion A reference to historical figures or events, fictional characters, place, or other things that the author assumes the reader will know and understand.

anachronism The representation of someone or something existing or happening in other than chronological, proper, or historical order.

comedy A form of literature in which characters are faced with moderate difficulties, but they overcome them and the story ends happily.

foreshadowing A literary technique using hints or clues that prepare the reader for something that might happen later in the work.

hyperbole Language that greatly overstates or exaggerates for rhetorical or comic effect.

irony Term indicating that the way something appears differs from reality, either in meaning, situation, or action.

metaphor A figure of speech that compares unlike objects without using connecting terms such as *like* or *as*.

oxymoron A statement that combines two terms usually seen as opposites. The effect created seems to be a contradiction, but is true. Some examples are *deafening silence; jumbo shrimp.*

personification A figure of speech in which objects or animals are given human qualities.

pun A play on words that has more than one meaning.

simile A figurative comparison using the words *like* or *as*. Some examples are *pretty as a picture; cunning like a fox.*

soliloquy A speech given in a drama, when characters speak their thoughts aloud while alone on stage, thereby communicating their thoughts, mental state, intentions, and motives to the audience.

tragedy A form of literature in which the hero is destroyed by a character flaw and a set of forces that cause the hero considerable suffering.

Many examples of these terms have been pointed out for you throughout this book. Pay attention and you may find even more!

Cast of characters or *Dramatis Personae*

Julius Caesar
A ruler of Rome

Calpurnia
Wife to Caesar

Cassius
Conspirator against Caesar

Brutus
Conspirator against Caesar

Portia
Wife to Brutus

Casca

**Caius
Ligarius**

**Decius
Brutus**

**Metellus
Cimber**

Cinna

All are conspirators against Julius Caesar

Octavius Caesar

Mark Antony

Triumvirs after the death of Julius Caesar

Lepidus

Flavius

Marullus

Roman Tribunes

**Artemidorus
of Cnidos**

A teacher of rhetoric

A Soothsayer

Cinna

A poet

Lucilius

Titinius

Messala

Young Cato

Volumnius

Friends to Brutus and Cassius

Flavius

vi

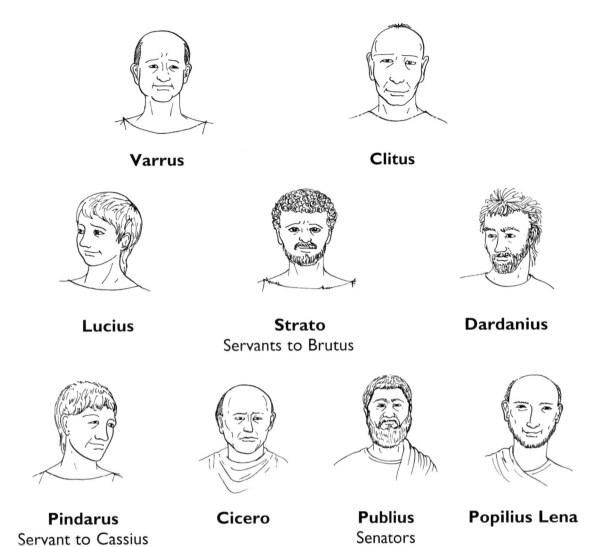

Varrus

Clitus

Lucius

Strato
Servants to Brutus

Dardanius

Pindarus
Servant to Cassius

Cicero

Publius
Senators

Popilius Lena

Settings of the Scenes:
- Rome, Italy
- Battlefield near Sardis
- Battlefield near Philippi

Act I Scene i	Two Roman **tribunes** named Flavius and Marullus meet a group of **plebeians** (or commoners) dressed in their finest clothes, lining a street on a typical work day in Rome.

Hence! Home, you idle creatures, get you home! Is this a holiday? Speak, what trade art thou?

Why, sir, a carpenter.

Literary terms

"Hence! Home you idle creatures" is an example of an **insult**; the cobbler uses a **pun**, or play upon the word "soul"—as in being a mender of human souls, not soles as in the bottoms of shoes.

Where is thy leather apron and thy rule? What dost thou with thy best apparel on?

Truly, sir, in respect of a fine workman, I am a cobbler.

You, sir, what trade are you?

But what trade art thou?

A trade, sir, that I hope I may use with a safe conscience, which is indeed, sir, a mender of bad soles.

tribune—an officer of ancient Rome who was elected to represent and to protect the rights of commoners
plebeians—commoners; the working class

1

The cobbler states that they are not working because they are awaiting Caesar's return to Rome. This angers the tribunes because Caesar killed Pompey, a fellow **triumvir** and Roman.

But why are you not in thy shop today? Why dost thou lead these men about the streets?

Truly, sir, to wear out their shoes, to get myself into more work. But indeed, sir, we make holiday to see Caesar, and to rejoice in his triumph.

Marullus: Wherefore rejoice? What conquest brings he home?
What **tributaries** follow him to Rome,
To grace in captive bonds his chariot wheels?
You blocks, you stones, you worse than senseless things!
O you hard hearts, you cruel men of Rome,
Knew you not Pompey? Many a time and oft
Have you climbed up to walls and battlements,
To towers and windows, yea, to chimney tops,
Your infants in your arms, and there have sat
The livelong day, with patient expectation,
To see great Pompey pass the streets of Rome
And when you saw his chariot but appear,
Have you not made an universal shout,
That **Tiber** trembled underneath her banks
To hear the replication of your sounds
Made in her concave shores?
And do you now put on your best attire?
And do you now **cull** out a holiday?
And do you now strew flowers in his way,
That comes in triumph over Pompey's blood?
Be gone! Run to your houses, fall upon your knees,
Pray to the gods to **intermit** the plague
That needs must light on this ingratitude.

Think about it

What is the meaning of loyalty? Should we remain loyal at all times, or can (or should) our loyalties change?

triumvirs—three men who jointly ruled Rome
tributaries—captives   Tiber—a river that flows through Rome
cull—choose to take; select, pick out   intermit—put off

<table>
<tr><td>**Act I Scene i**</td><td>After Marullus' angry speech, Flavius sends the commoners away. The tribunes will remove the decorations that Caesar's followers have placed around the city to keep Caesar equal with humans and not above them like the gods.</td></tr>
</table>

Go, go, good countrymen, and weep your tears into the channel. Go!

Go you down that way towards the Capitol, this way will I. Disrobe the images, if you do find them decked with ceremonies.

May we do so? You know it is the **Feast of Lupercal**.

Let no images be hung with Caesar's **trophies**. These growing feathers plucked from Caesar's wing will make him fly an ordinary **pitch**, who else would soar above the view of men, and keep us all in servile fearfulness.

Feast of Lupercal—a fertility festival that was celebrated on February 15th
trophies—ornaments in honor of Caesar
pitch—the highest point of a hawk's flight

Act I Scene ii

Julius Caesar arrives in Rome with an **entourage**. Caesar asks Antony to touch Calpurnia during his run and then Caesar hears the voice of someone calling him. It is a Soothsayer who tells him to "**beware the ides of March.**"

Forget not to touch Calpurnia, for our elders say the barren, touchéd in this holy chase, shake off their sterile curse.

I shall remember.

Who calls? Who is it in the **press** that calls on me? I hear a tongue, shriller than all the music. Speak.

Beware the ides of March.

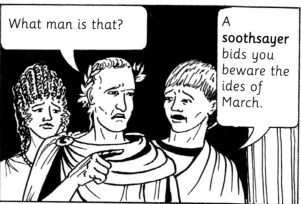

What man is that?

A **soothsayer** bids you beware the ides of March.

He is a dreamer. Let us leave him—pass.

Think about it

If a stranger walked up to you and told you to beware of something, how would you react? Would you take it seriously or ignore it completely?

entourage—a group of people following or attending an important person
the ides of March—March 15th according to the Roman calendar
press—the crowd of people   **soothsayer**—a person who makes predictions about the future

4

Caesar and the crowd have moved on, but Brutus and Cassius remain behind. Cassius notices Brutus' troubled looks and asks why Brutus doesn't see his own strengths as others do.

Brutus, I do observe you lately and have not seen that gentleness and show of love from your eyes.

Be not deceived. If I have **veiled** my look, I turn the troubled **countenance** merely upon myself.

Think about It

How do others perceive us? Do we see ourselves the same way that others do?

It is much **lamented**, Brutus, that you cannot see your hidden worthiness. Many of the best respect in Rome, speaking of Brutus, **have wished that Brutus had his eyes**.

veiled—to disguise or cover
countenance—facial expression
lamented—to grieve for or regret deeply
have wished that Brutus had his eyes—many wished that Brutus could see himself the way they see him—as being worthy of crowned king

<table>
<tr><td>**Act 1
Scene ii**</td><td>Brutus reacts to the cheering and agrees with Cassius that he does not want to have Caesar crowned king. Cassius tells Brutus two stories that prove Caesar's weakness and inability to lead well.</td></tr>
</table>

Brutus: What means this shouting? I do fear the people
Choose Caesar for their king.

Cassius: Ay, do you fear it?
Then I must think you would not have it so.

Brutus: I would not Cassius, yet I love him well.
But what is it that you would impart to me?
If it be aught toward the general good,
Set honor in one eye and death in the other
And I will look on both **indifferently**;
For let the gods so speed me as I love
The name of honor more than I fear death.

indifferently—impartially

Cassius: I know that virtue to be in you, Brutus,
Well, honor is the subject of my story.
I cannot tell what you and other men
Think of this life; but, for my single self,
I was born free as Caesar; so were you;
And we can both endure the winter's cold as well as he.
For once, upon a raw and gusty day,
Caesar said to me "Dar'st thou, Cassius, now
Leap in with me into this angry flood
And swim to yonder point?" Upon the word
I plungèd in and bade him to follow; so indeed he did.

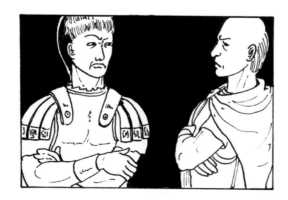

The torrent roared but ere we could arrive at the point proposed,
Caesar cried "Help me, Cassius, or I sink!"
I as Aeneas, our great ancestor,
Did from the flames of Troy upon his shoulder
The old Anchises bear, so from the Tiber
Did I the tired Caesar. And this man
Is now become a god, and Cassius is
A wretched creature and must **bend his body**
If Caesar carelessly but nod on him.
He had a fever when he was in Spain,
And when the **fit** was on him, I did mark
How he did shake. 'Tis true, this god did shake.
His coward lips did from their color fly,
And that same eye whose bend doth awe the world
Did lose his luster. I did hear him groan.
You gods, it doth amaze me that a man of such feeble temper should
So get the start of the majestic world
And bear the palm alone.

bend his body—to bow at the foot of an important person

fit—an epileptic seizure

And bear the palm alone—carry the prize, or a sign of victory, on his own

---

Literary terms

Shakespeare uses an **allusion**, or reference to mythology (the Trojan hero Aeneas who carried his father to safety on his shoulders) to demonstrate how strong Cassius was in rescuing Caesar from the Tiber River.

| **Act I Scene ii** | Hearing more shouting, Brutus and Cassius assume the crowd is honoring Caesar. Cassius wonders how Caesar has come to be so respected and continues to talk about **fate**. Brutus responds to Cassius and admits that he would rather be a **villager** than a citizen of Rome under the present conditions. |

Another shout! I do believe that these applauses are for some new honors heaped on Caesar.

Why he doth bestride the narrow world like a **Colossus,** and we petty men walk under his huge legs.

Men at some time are the masters of their fates. The fault, dear Brutus, is not in our stars, but in ourselves, that we are underlings.

Brutus and Caesar—What should be in that "Caesar?" Why should that name be sounded more than yours? Upon what **meat** doth this our Caesar feed that he is grown so great?

How I have thought of this, and of these times. For this situation I would not be encouraged. What you have said I will consider and answer, but until then, my noble friend, **chew upon this:** Brutus had rather be a **villager** than to repute himself a son of Rome under these conditions as time is like to lay upon us.

Think about it

Is our fate really in our own hands? Do we decide our own future or is there more to it than that?

---

fate—destiny; outcome of one's life   **villager**—a peasant
Colossus—the Colossus of Rhodes is a giant bronze statue that straddled the entrance to the harbor—ships were able to pass underneath.
meat—food   **chew upon this**—think about, consider

Caesar returns with his entourage and notices Cassius' "lean and hungry look"—a look that Caesar believes to be dangerous. But Antony reassures him that Cassius is an honorable Roman.

Antonius!

Caesar?

Yond Cassius has a lean and hungry look. He thinks too much. Such men are dangerous.

He reads much, he is a great observer, and looks through the deeds of men. He loves no plays, he **hears no music.** Seldom does he smile and such men will never be at heart's ease while they behold a greater than themselves, and therefore are they very dangerous.

Fear him not, Caesar. He's not dangerous. He is a **noble** Roman.

hears no music—someone who has no music within himself cannot be trusted—and could be capable of treason or disloyalty
noble—honorable, trustworthy

As Caesar and his entourage leave, Casca remains behind to speak to Brutus and Cassius. He tells them that Caesar, who was offered the king's crown three times, refused it.

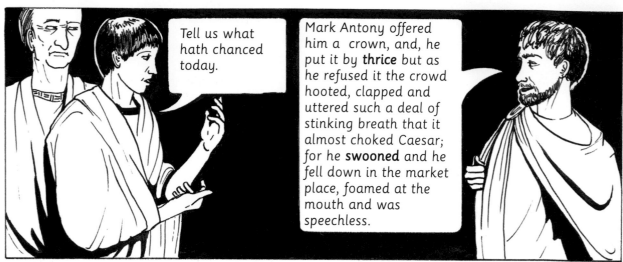

Tell us what hath chanced today.

Mark Antony offered him a crown, and, he put it by **thrice** but as he refused it the crowd hooted, clapped and uttered such a deal of stinking breath that it almost choked Caesar; for he **swooned** and he fell down in the market place, foamed at the mouth and was speechless.

Did Cicero say any thing?

Aye, he spoke Greek. But those that understood him smiled at one another and shook their heads—but for mine own part, *it was Greek to me*.

Think about it

Have you ever listened to someone speak or tried to read something that made no sense at all and felt as Casca did—that "it was Greek" to you?

thrice—three times
swooned—fainted

Cassius reveals that despite Brutus' noble spirit or temperament, he believes that Brutus can be persuaded to change his mind about Caesar, and he will write letters as though they were from different citizens to convince Brutus for the betterment of Rome.

Cassius: Well, Brutus, thou art noble. Yet I see
Thy honorable **mettle** may be **wrought**
From that it is **disposed**. Therefore it is meet
That noble minds keep ever with their likes;
For who so **firm** that cannot be seduced?
Caesar **doth bear me hard**, but he loves Brutus.
If I were Brutus now, and he were Cassius,
He should not **humor** me. I will this night,
In several hands, in at his windows throw,
As if they came from several citizens,
Writings, all tending to the great opinion
That Rome holds of his name, wherein obscurely
Caesar's ambition shall be **glancèd at**.
And after this, let Caesar **seat him sure**,
For we will **shake** him, or worse days endure.

mettle—temperament, spirit
wrought . . . disposed—worked on or changed

firm—stubborn
doth bear me hard—holds a grudge against

humor—influence

glancèd at—mentioned
seat him sure—seat himself securely
shake—remove him from his dominant position

Literary terms

Shakespeare uses a **soliloquy** to call attention to Cassius' plans to convince Brutus to help him remove Caesar from his position.

Think about it

According to Cassius, how does Caesar feel about him? How does Caesar feel about Brutus? What does Cassius plan to do that night in order to influence Brutus?

<table>
<tr><td>**Act I Scene iii**</td><td>Casca and Cicero meet on a street with a frightening thunder and lightning storm in the background. Many strange things have been occurring and Casca believes that these strange incidents are omens of danger.</td></tr>
</table>

Good evening, Casca, why are you breathless and why stare you so?

O Cicero, I have seen tempests when the **scolding winds** have **rived** the knotty oaks, and I have seen the **ambitious ocean** swell and rage and foam, but never till tonight did I witness such strange signs.

When these **prodigies** do meet I believe they are omens of dangerous happenings to come.

Indeed, it is a **strange-disposèd** time. This disturbed sky is not to walk in.

Literary terms

Personification is used to draw attention to the strength of the winds and the ocean in a storm. **Foreshadowing** is used to hint at what might occur in the future when Casca points out that these strange sightings are omens.

rived—split
prodigies—ghostly sights, omens
strange-disposèd—abnormal

<table>
<tr><td>

**Act I
Scene iii**

</td><td>

Cassius arrives and tells Casca that the heavens are using this storm and the unusual events as warnings of far more serious consequences—meaning that if Caesar is crowned king, worse things will happen.

</td></tr>
</table>

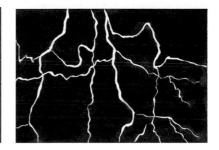

Casca: Who ever knew the heavens menace so?

Cassius: Those that have known the earth so full of faults.
For my part, I have walked about the streets,
Submitting me unto the perilous night,
And thus **unbracèd**, Casca, as you see,   **unbracèd**—shirt opened
Have bared my bosom to the thunder-stone;
And when the cross blue lightning seemed to open
The breast of heaven, I did present myself
Even in the aim and very flash of it.

Casca: But wherefore did you so much tempt the heavens?
It is the part of men to fear and tremble
When the most mighty gods by tokens send
Such dreadful heralds to **astonish** us.   **astonish**—stun with fear

Cassius: You are dull, Casca, and those sparks of life
That should be in a Roman you do want.
But if you would consider the true cause,
You shall find that heaven hath infused them with these spirits
To make them instruments of fear and warning
Unto some monstrous state.

Think about it

Today with the advancement of science, we know how thunder and lightning occur, but in ancient Rome, such things were believed to be caused by the gods. What might the underlying reason be for thunder and lightning?

13

Casca: 'Tis Caesar that you mean, is it not, Cassius?
Indeed they say the Senators tomorrow
Mean to establish Caesar as a king,
And he shall wear his crown in every place save here in Italy.

Cassius: I know where I will wear this dagger then;
Cassius from bondage will deliver Cassius.
Therein, ye gods, you make the weak most strong;
Therein, ye gods, you tyrants do defeat.
Nor stony tower, nor wall of beaten brass,
Nor airless dungeon, nor strong links of iron,
Can be retentive to the strength of spirit;
But life, being weary of these worldly bars
Never lacks power to dismiss itself.
If I know this, know all the world besides,
That part of tyranny that I do bear
I can shake off at pleasure.

Casca: So can I:
So every bondman in his own hand bears
The power to cancel his captivity.

Cassius: Now know you, Casca,
I have **moved** already
Some certain of the noblest-minded Romans
To undergo with me an enterprise
Of honorable-dangerous consequence.
And I do know, **by this** they stay for me
In **Pompey's porch**. For now, this fearful night,
There is no stir or walking in the streets;
And the complexion of the element
Is favored, like the work we have in hand,
Most bloody, fiery, and most terrible.

moved—persuaded

by this—by now
Pompey's Porch—the portico (colonnade) opposite Pompey's Theater

Cinna arrives looking for Cassius because the other conspirators are waiting for him. He pleads with him to win Brutus' allegiance to their plan against Caesar. Cassius replies that it is midnight, and Brutus will be on their side by morning.

Stand **close** for here comes one in haste.

Tis Cinna...he is a friend. Cinna, where haste you so?

To find out you.

O Cassius, if you could win the noble Brutus to our party—

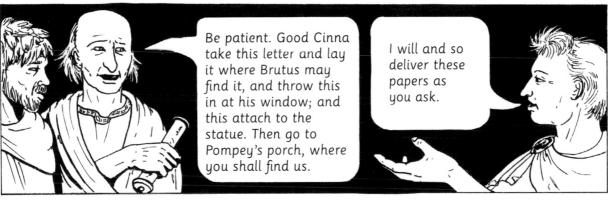

Be patient. Good Cinna take this letter and lay it where Brutus may find it, and throw this in at his window; and this attach to the statue. Then go to Pompey's porch, where you shall find us.

I will and so deliver these papers as you ask.

Brutus sits high in all the people's hearts, we need his virtue and support on our side.

Come Casca, you and I will yet **ere day** see Brutus at his house. Three parts of him is ours already. Let us go, for it is after midnight, and ere day we will awake him and be sure of him.

close—hidden
ere day—before day comes

**Act II
Scene i**

Early in the morning of the 15th of March, the ides of March,
Brutus considers the effect that the power of being crowned king
would have, and how this power would turn Caesar into a tyrant.

Brutus: It must be by his death and for my part
I know no personal cause to **spurn** at him,
But for the general. He would be crowned:
How that might change his nature, there's the question.
It is the bright day that brings forth the **adder**,
And that craves wary walking. Crown him that—
And then, I grant, we **put a sting in him**
That at his will he may do danger with.
The abuse of greatness is when it disjoins
Remorse from power. And, to speak truth of Caesar,
I have not known when his affections swayed
More than his reason. But 'tis a common proof
That *lowliness is young ambition's ladder*,
Whereto the climber-upward turns his face;
But when he once attains the upmost round,
He then unto the ladder turns his back,
Looks in the clouds, scorning the base degrees
By which he did ascend. So Caesar may.
Then, lest he may, prevent. And since the quarrel
Will bear no color for the thing he is,
Fashion it thus: that what he is, **augmented**,
Would run to these and these extremities.
And therefore think him as a serpent's egg,
Which, hatched, would, as his kind, grow **mischievous**,
And kill him in the shell.

spurn—strike out

adder—a poisonous snake

put a sting in him—make him mean or vicious

Literary terms
A **metaphor** comparing ambition to climbing a ladder

augmented—to increase or empower

mischievous—harmful

Think about it
Do you agree or disagree with the notion that success and power cause people to change?

Act II Scene i Brutus is given a letter by his servant that is similar to the one he received earlier, suggesting that Brutus be more aware of his powers. Noting that it is the ides of March, or March 15th, there is a sudden knocking at the door. All of the conspirators arrive.

Get me a **taper** in my study, Lucius.

Is not tomorrow, boy, the ides of March?

Searching for a **flint**, I found this paper and I am sure it did not lie there earlier. And, sir, March is wasted fifteen days.

The **exhalations** whizzing in the air
Give so much light that I may read by them.

*"Brutus thou sleep'st. Awake and see thyself. Shall Rome, etc., [stand under one man's awe?] Speak, strike, **redress**."*

Am I entreated to speak and strike?
O Rome, I make thee promise, if the redress will follow, thou receivest thy full petition at the hand of Brutus!

taper—a candle
flint—a stone used to light a fire
exhalations—meteors
etc.—Shakespeare did not add the words of the letter to the script. A letter was given to the actor to read
redress—the remedy or to set something right

Brutus greets the conspirators and they agree to continue with the plot against Caesar. Cassius argues that perhaps they should murder Mark Antony as well because he is well-liked by Caesar. But Brutus disagrees.

Give me your hands all over, one by one.

And let us swear our resolution.

No, not an oath. What other bond than secret Romans that have spoke the word, and will not **palter**?

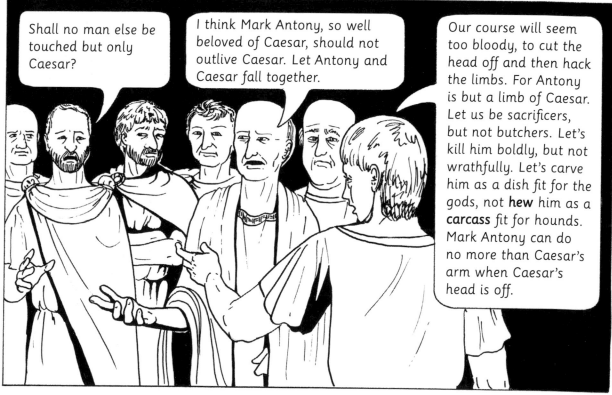

Shall no man else be touched but only Caesar?

I think Mark Antony, so well beloved of Caesar, should not outlive Caesar. Let Antony and Caesar fall together.

Our course will seem too bloody, to cut the head off and then hack the limbs. For Antony is but a limb of Caesar. Let us be sacrificers, but not butchers. Let's kill him boldly, but not wrathfully. Let's carve him as a dish fit for the gods, not **hew** him as a **carcass** fit for hounds. Mark Antony can do no more than Caesar's arm when Caesar's head is off.

palter—waver, shift, or change position
hew—to chop up
carcass—a dead body

Brutus: Peace! Count the *clock*.

Cassius: The clock hath stricken three

Trebonius: 'Tis time to part

Cassius: But it is doubtful yet
Whether Caesar will come forth today or no,
For he is superstitious grown of late,
Quite from the main opinion he held once
Of fantasy, of dreams and ceremonies.
It may be these **apparent prodigies**,
The unaccustomed terror of this night
And the persuasion of his **augurers**,
May hold him form the Capitol today.

Decius: Never fear that. If he be so resolved,
I can o'ersway him. For he loves to hear
That *unicorns may be betrayed with trees*
And bears with glasses, elephants with holes,
Lions with toils and men with flatterers.
He says he does, being then most flattered.
Let me work,
For I can give his humor the true bent,
And I will bring him to the Capitol.

Brutus: By the eighth hour. . .
Good gentlemen, look fresh and merrily.
Let not our looks put on our purposes,
But bear it as our Roman actors do,
With untired spirits and formal constancy.
And so, good morrow to you every one.

> **Literary terms**
> Although there were no striking clocks during Caesar's era, Shakespeare used the clock to indicate time. This is an **anachronism**.

apparent prodigies—conspicuous omens

augurers—augurs (Roman religious officials whose function was to predict future events)

> **Literary terms**
> An allusion to mythology is used here to illustrate how cleverly Decius can persuade or trick Caesar into going to the Senate. It was believed that the unicorn was tricked by the lion who would stand in front of a tree and provoke the unicorn to charge at him, the lion would step aside, and the unicorn's horn would be impaled into the tree, making the unicorn easy prey for the clever lion.

> **Think about it**
> Have you ever heard of the saying, a cliché, that "flattery will get you nowhere"? What is flattery? How does flattery work? Is it a good thing or can it be a negative?

Brutus' wife Portia enters the room just as the men leave. She is worried about Brutus and questions him about his mood and behavior. Brutus replies that it is simply because of his health, when there is a sudden knock at the door.

Portia: Brutus, my lord!

Brutus: Portia, what mean you? Wherefore rise you now?

Portia: You've ungently, Brutus
Stole from my bed. And yesternight at supper
You suddenly arose and walked about,
Musing and sighing, with your arms across.
And when I asked you what the matter was,
You stared upon me with ungentle looks.
I urged you further, then you scratched your head,
And too impatiently stamped with your foot.
Yet I insisted, yet you answered not,
But with an angry **wafture** of your hand
Gave sign for me to leave you. So I did…
Dear my lord, Make me acquainted with your cause of grief.

musing—concerned or deep thinking

wafture—wave

Brutus: I am not well in health, and that is all.

Portia: Brutus is wise, and were he not in health,
He would embrace the means to come by it.
No, my Brutus; You have some sick offense within your mind.
Which by the right and virtue of my place
Within the bond of marriage, tell me, Brutus,
It is excepted I should know no secrets
That appertain to you?
     [knock at the door]

> **Think about it**
>
> Intuition—the power or ability to know things without a conscious reasoning. Would you agree that Portia has a strong intuition regarding her husband? Should we pay attention to our intuitions?

Brutus: O you gods. Render me worthy of this noble wife!
Hark, hark! One knocks. Portia, go in a while,
Leave me with haste. *[Portia exits]*

[Enter Lucius and Ligarius]

Lucius: Here is a sick man that would speak with you

Ligarius: I am not sick, if Brutus have in hand
Any exploit worth the name of honor.

Brutus: Such an exploit have I in hand, Ligarius,
Had you a healthful ear to hear of it.
A piece of work that will make sick men whole.
I shall unfold to thee as we are going
To whom it must be done.

Think about it

What does Brutus mean when he says, "A piece of work that will make sick men whole?

Act II Scene ii

Calpurnia, Caesar's wife, begs Caesar not to go to the Senate today because of her dreams and other strange events. But Decius Brutus arrives to escort Caesar to the Senate assuring them that they have misinterpreted the meaning of the dreams. He states that if Caesar does not go, he will be thought a weak leader.

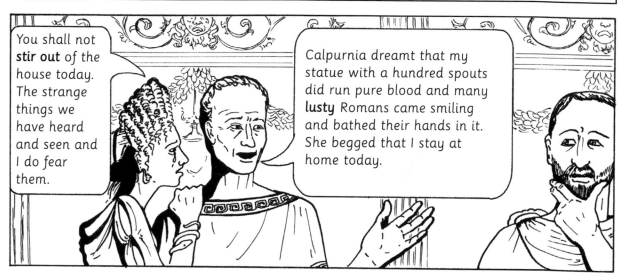

You shall not **stir out** of the house today. The strange things we have heard and seen and I do fear them.

Calpurnia dreamt that my statue with a hundred spouts did run pure blood and many **lusty** Romans came smiling and bathed their hands in it. She begged that I stay at home today.

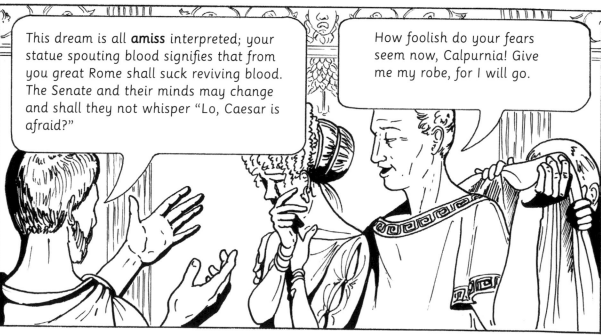

This dream is all **amiss** interpreted; your statue spouting blood signifies that from you great Rome shall suck reviving blood. The Senate and their minds may change and shall they not whisper "Lo, Caesar is afraid?"

How foolish do your fears seem now, Calpurnia! Give me my robe, for I will go.

stir out—leave from
lusty—joyful
amiss—wrongly

Artemidorus, a teacher and a friend of several of the conspirators (he therefore knows of their plan to murder Caesar) reads a letter that he has written for Caesar warning him of the danger that awaits him.

Here will I stand till Caesar pass along, and as a **suitor** will I give him this, if thou read this, O Caesar, thou may live; if not, **the Fates** with traitors do **contrive**.

"Caesar, beware of Brutus; take heed of Cassius; come not near Casca; have an eye to Cinna; trust not Trebonius; mark well Metellus Cimber, Decius Brutus loves thee not, thou hast wronged Caius Ligarius. There is but one mind in all these men, and it is bent against Caesar. If thou beest not immortal, look about you. Security gives way to conspiracy. The mighty gods defend thee!"

Thy lover, Artemidorus

suitor—someone who presents a petition
the Fates from mythology, the three goddesses who directed the destinies of humans
contrive—to plot against

Portia sends one of their servants to the Senate to check on Brutus when a Soothsayer passes on his way to the Senate to speak with Caesar. Portia asks if he is aware of any harm that is intended for Caesar. The Soothsayer states that he is aware of none, but still fears for Caesar.

I **prithee** boy, run to the Senate House and bring me word if thy lord look well, for he went sickly forth.

Thou hast some **suit** to Caesar, hast thou not?

That I have lady. If Caesar will hear me, I shall **beseech** him to **befriend** himself.

Do you know of any harm intended toward him?

None, that I know will be, much that I fear may chance.

prithee—pray thee
suit—petition
beseech—to ask
befriend—to be kind to, to favor

Act III Scene i	Caesar approaches the Senate and dismisses both the Soothsayer and Artemidorus. Casca is the first to stab Caesar, followed by the rest of the conspirators. Caesar, shocked that Brutus is involved, falls dead.

Think about it

Et tu, Brutè? are Caesar's last words. It is a comment of disbelief in discovering that Brutus, someone whom Caesar admired, could be involved in the conspiracy against him. Think about this scene and Caesar's last words. Consider the strength of the emotion not only with Caesar, but with every person involved.

schedule—a document
Et tu, Brutè?—And thou, Brutus? A well-known comment or phrase that is associated with Caesar's assassination

The conspirators are eager to celebrate the death of Caesar. Antony sends word to Brutus that he will follow Brutus as he once did Caesar. Because of this promise, Antony is given permission to speak at Caesar's funeral. Antony is told of Octavius' arrival.

Liberty! Freedom! **Tyranny** is dead! Run hence, proclaim, cry it about the streets.

People, and Senators stand still. Ambition's debt is paid.

Let us bathe our hands in Caesar's blood up to the elbows, and **besmear** our swords. Then walk to the marketplace waving our red weapons o'er our heads and cry "Peace, freedom, and liberty!"

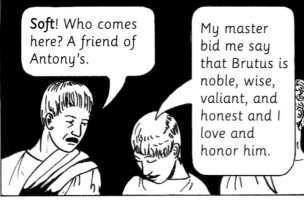

Soft! Who comes here? A friend of Antony's.

My master bid me say that Brutus is noble, wise, valiant, and honest and I love and honor him.

But here comes Antony, welcome.

Friends, I am with you, may I bring his body to the marketplace and speak in the order of his funeral.

Caesar wrote to him to come to Rome. He is within seven leagues.

Return quickly and tell him what happened, Rome is in mourning and too dangerous.

tyranny—unjust and severe rule
besmear— to soil or to smear onto
soft—stop, hold it

Brutus' simple and passionless speech informs the citizens that Caesar was killed because of his ambition and their fear of becoming slaves under his rule. Mark Antony then enters with Caesar's body. Brutus asks that everyone stay and listen.

Brutus: Be patient till the last.
Romans, countrymen, and lovers, bear me for my cause, and be silent, that you may hear. Believe me for mine honor, and have respect to mine honor that you may believe. Censure me in your wisdom and awake your senses, that you may the better judge. If there be any in this assembly, any dear friend of Caesar's, to him I say that Brutus' love to Caesar was no less than his. If then that friend demand why Brutus rose against Caesar, this is my answer: not that I loved Caesar less, but that I loved Rome more. Had you rather Caesar were living, and die all slaves, than that Caesar were dead, to live all freemen? As Caesar loved me, I weep for him. As he was fortunate, I rejoice as it. As he was valiant, I honor him. But—as he was ambitious, I slew him. There is tears for his love, joy for his fortune, honor for his valor, and death for his ambition. Who is here so base that would be a **bondman**? If any, speak, for him I have offended. Who is here so rude that would not be a Roman? If any, speak; for him have I offended. I pause for a reply.

bondman—slave

All: None, Brutus none!

Think about it

"There is tears for his love; joy for his fortune; honor for his valor, and death for his ambition." Ambition—Caesar was killed because of this ambition. Do you agree or disagree with Brutus' reasoning?

Brutus: Then none have I offended. I have done no more to Caesar than you shall do to Brutus.

[Mark Antony and others enter with Caesar's body.]

Here come his body, mourned by Mark Antony,
who, though he had no hand in his death, shall
receive the benefit of his dying—a place in the
commonwealth—as which of you shall not? With
this I depart: that, as I slew my best **lover** for the   lover—friend
good of Rome, I have the same dagger for myself
when it shall please my country to need my death.
Good countrymen, let me depart alone,
And, for my sake, stay here with Antony.
Do grace to Caesar's corpse, and grace his speech
Tending to Caesar's glories, which Mark Antony
(By our permission) is allowed to make.
I do entreat you, not a man depart,
Save I alone, till Antony have spoke.

[Brutus leaves]

Think about it

Is Brutus believable when he tries to convince the Roman crowd that the conspirators killed Caesar for a good cause?

Act III Scene ii	Antony begins one of the most famous and powerful speeches in literature. Although Antony begins by saying that he has come to bury Caesar, not to praise him, that is exactly what he does—praise Caesar.	

Antony: Friends, Romans, countrymen, lend me your ears.
I come to bury Caesar, not to praise him.
The evil that men do lives after them;
The good is oft **interred** with their bones.

interred—buried with

So let it be with Caesar. The noble Brutus
Hath told you Caesar was ambitious.
If it were so, it was a grievous fault,
And grievously hath Caesar answered it.
Here under leave of Brutus and the rest
(For Brutus is an honorable man;
So are they all, all honorable men),
Come I to speak in Caesar's funeral.
He was my friend, faithful and just to me,
But Brutus says he was ambitious,
And Brutus is an honorable man.
He hath brought many captives home to Rome,
Whose ransoms did the general coffers fill.
Did this in Caesar seem ambitious?
When that the poor have cried, Caesar hath wept;
Ambition should be made of sterner stuff.

Literary terms

Irony is used repeatedly throughout Antony's speech when he refers to Brutus as being an "honorable man."

29

Yet Brutus says he was ambitious;
And Brutus is an honorable man.
You all did see that on the Lupercal
I thrice presented him a kingly crown,
Which he did thrice refuse. Was this ambition?
Yet Brutus says he was ambitious,
And sure he is an honorable man.
I speak not to disprove what Brutus spoke,
But here I am to speak what I do know.
You all did love him once, not without cause.
What cause withholds you then to mourn for him?
O judgment, thou art fled to brutish beasts,
And men have lost their reason! Bear with me.
My heart is in the coffin there with Caesar,
And I must pause till it come back to me.

Think about it

After hearing each of the positive qualities of Caesar in Antony's speech, followed by the repeated statement that "Brutus is an honorable man," do you think that the citizens of Rome will understand Antony's hidden meaning?

In continuing his speech, Antony tells the crowd that he does not want to wrong Brutus and Cassius (who are honorable men), but that if the citizens were to hear what Caesar has written in his will, they would be furious and enraged.

Antony: But yesterday the word of Caesar might
Have stood against the world. Now lies he there,
And none so poor to do him reverence
O masters; If I were disposed to stir
Your hearts and minds to mutiny and rage,
I should do Brutus wrong, and Cassius wrong,
Who, you all know are honorable men.
I will not do them wrong. I rather choose
To wrong the dead, to wrong myself and you,
Than I will wrong such honorable men.
But here's a parchment with the seal of Caesar.
I found it in his closet. 'Tis his will.
Let but the commons hear this testament,
Which (pardon me) I do not mean to read,

All: The will, the will! We will hear Caesar's will!

Antony: Have patience, gentle friends; I must not read it.
It is not **meet** you know how Caesar loved you.   meet—proper, right
You are not wood, you are not stones, but men;
And being men, hearing the will of Caesar,
It will inflame you, it will make you mad.
'Tis good you know not that you are his heirs,
For if you should, O, what would come of it?
You will compel me, then, to read the will?
Then make a ring about the corpse of Caesar,
And let me show you him that made the will.

Think about it

Is Antony really supporting Brutus, or only pretending to so that he can use this opportunity to turn the Roman people against Brutus, Cassius, and the other conspirators?

If you have tears, prepare to shed them now.
You all do know this **mantle.**   mantle—cloak, clothing
Look, in this place ran Cassius' dagger through.
See what a **rent** the envious Casca made.   rent—hole, rip
Through this the well belovèd Brutus stabbed,
And, as he plucked his cursèd steel away,
Mark how the blood of Caesar followed it,
For Brutus, as you know, was Caesar's angel.
Judge, O you gods, how dearly Caesar loved him!
This was **the most unkindest cut of all.***
For when the noble Caesar saw him stab
Ingratitude, more strong than traitors' arms,
Quite **vanquished** him. Then burst his mighty heart,   vanquished—to overcome
And great Caesar fell.

Think about it

*A well-known quote, the wound Caesar suffered from Brutus is the source of the most pain—*the most unkindest cut of all.* How does Antony explain Caesar's fondness of Brutus?

Antony concludes ironically by stating that although he is not the orator or speaker that Brutus is, he wishes he had the power of speech that would "stir men's blood." Antony then reads Caesar's will and this enrages the citizens.

Antony: Good friends, sweet friends, let me not stir you up
To such a sudden flood of mutiny.
They that have done this deed are honorable.
What private griefs they have, alas, I know not,
That made them do it. They are wise and honorable
And will no doubt with reason answer you.
I come not, friends, to steal away your hearts.
I am no orator, as Brutus is,
But, as you know me all, a plain blunt man
That love my friend, and that they know full well
That gave me public leave to speak of him.
For I have neither wit, nor word, nor worth,
Action, nor utterance, nor the power of speech
To stir men's blood. I only speak right on.
I tell you that which you yourselves do know,
Show you sweet Caesar's wounds, poor poor **dumb mouths**,   **dumb mouths**—unable to speak
And bid them speak for me. But were I Brutus,
And Brutus Antony, there were an Antony
Would ruffle up your spirits, and put a tongue
In every wound of Caesar that should move
The stones of Rome to rise and mutiny.

All: We'll mutiny.

Think about it

What is your opinion of Antony's speech? Was he able to stir their blood, or was it a passionless speech that put them all to sleep? Explain.

Antony: Why, friends, you go to do you know not what.
Wherein hath Caesar thus deserved your loves?
Alas, you know not! I must tell you then.
You have forgot the will I told you of.
Here is the will, and under Caesar's seal.
To every Roman citizen he gives,
To every several man, seventy-five **drachmas**.
Moreover he hath left you all his walks,
His private arbors, and new-planted orchard,
On this side Tiber. He hath left them you,
And to your heirs forever—common pleasures
To walk abroad and **recreate** yourselves.
Here was a Caesar! When comes such another?

Citizen: Never, never! Come away, away!
We'll burn the body in the holy place
And with the brands fire the traitors' houses.
Take up the body.

drachmas—silver coins

recreate—recreation, divert oneself

Think about it

What is your opinion of Julius Caesar after Antony has read his will? Has your opinion of him changed?

Antony is certain that the angry citizens will do what is needed, which is to remove the conspirators. Octavius has arrived in Rome and is at Caesar's home. Brutus and Cassius have fled the city.

afoot—in action, in motion

Cinna, the poet, is on his way to Caesar's funeral, when he is questioned by a few enraged citizens who mistake him for Cinna, the conspirator. Although Cinna declares that he is a poet, the angry group murders him unjustly.

I dreamt **tonight** that I did feast with Caesar, and things **charge my fantasy**.

What is your name?

Where are you going?

Where do you dwell?

Are you a married man or a bachelor?

Your name, sir, truly.

Truly, my name is Cinna.

I am Cinna the poet!

It is no matter; his name's Cinna! Pluck but his name out of his heart, and turn him going.

Tear him to pieces! He's a conspirator.

Think about it

What is the meaning of "Mob mentality?"

tonight—last night
charge my fantasy—burden my imagination with bad omens

36

A new Triumvirate has been formed. The three men are discussing whom among their enemies should be killed and if there is a way to reduce the amount of money that Caesar left to the citizens of Rome. Antony also reports that Brutus and Cassius are gathering an army.

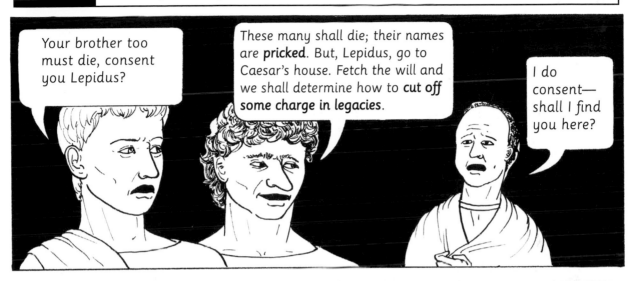

Your brother too must die, consent you Lepidus?

These many shall die; their names are **pricked**. But, Lepidus, go to Caesar's house. Fetch the will and we shall determine how to **cut off some charge in legacies**.

I do consent—shall I find you here?

Brutus and Cassius are levying powers, therefore let our alliance be combined, and let us go resolve how best to approach this matter.

Let us for we are **at the stake and bayed about** with many enemies; some that smile have in their hearts, I fear, millions of **mischiefs**.

pricked—marked for death with a pin prick
cut off some charge in legacies—to reduce the payment promised by Caesar
at the stake and bayed about—an Elizabethan sport—a bear is tied to a stake and dogs bay (howl/bark) at it
mischiefs—hostile thoughts or actions

Think about it

Caesar left a great deal of money to the citizens of Rome —and now the new Triumvirate is attempting to reduce that sum; how are the citizens going to respond?

| Act IV Scene ii | Brutus is camping with his army and sends for Cassius. They discuss future plans inside Brutus' tent so that the armies will not see them argue. |  |

Stand ho!

Most noble brother, you have done me wrong. Brutus, this sober form of yours hides wrongs; And when you do them—

Judge me, you gods! wrong I mine enemies? And if not so, how should I wrong a brother?

Cassius be content. Speak your griefs softly. Before the eyes of both our armies here—let us not wrangle. Bid them move away. Then in my tent, enlarge your griefs, and I will give you audience.

Pindarus, bid our commanders lead their charges off a little from this ground.

sober—serious manner
griefs—complaints, criticisms
wrangle—argue

Think about it

There is obviously some tension here between Brutus and Cassius; why would Brutus suggest that they discuss their plans away from the men?

Cassius: Brutus, **bait** not me!
I'll not endure it. You forget yourself
To **hedge** me in. I am a soldier, I,
Older in practice, abler than yourself
To make **conditions.**

bait—harass

hedge—to enclose, to fence in

conditions—term of a contract

Brutus: Go to! You are not, Cassius.

Cassius: I am.

Brutus: I say you are not.

Cassius: Do not presume too much upon my love.
I may do that I shall be sorry for.

Brutus: You have done what you should be sorry for.
There is no terror, Cassius, in your threats,
For I am armed so strong in honesty
That they pass by me as the idle wind,
Which I respect not.

> **Think about it**
> Why does Cassius seem to be so stressed or frustrated? How does Brutus respond to Cassius' mood?

Cassius: Antony and young Octavius are coming!
Revenge yourselves alone on Cassius.
For Cassius is aweary of the world—
Hated by one he loves, **braved** by his brother,
Checked like a **bondman**, all his faults observed,
There is my dagger,
And here my naked breast; strike as thou didst at Caesar,
For I know, when thou didst hate him worst, thou lovedst him better
Than ever thou lovedst Cassius.

braved—to be bullied
bondman—slave

Brutus: Sheathe your dagger.
Be angry when you will; it shall have **scope**.
O Cassius, you are yokèd with a lamb
That carries anger as the flint bears fire,
Who, **much enforcèd,** shows a hasty spark,
And straight is cold again.

scope—room to move

Cassius: O Brutus!

much enforcéd—struck hard (in reference to the flint); strongly provoked (in reference to his lamblike self)

Brutus: What's the matter?

Cassius: Have not you love enough to bear with me
When that **rash humor** which my mother gave me
Makes me forgetful?

rash humor—anger

Brutus: Yes, Cassius; and from henceforth
When you are over-earnest with your Brutus,
He'll think your mother **chides**, and leave you so.

chides—to scold

Think about it

When Cassius describes his "rash humor that my mother gave me," is he describing a characteristic or effeminate trait in himself inherited from his mother?

Act IV Scene iii	Brutus explains that his wife Portia has committed suicide. Titinius and Messala enter into the discussion and report that Octavius and Antony have killed more than 100 senators. They are readying their armies and will soon be marching toward Philippi.

I did not think you could have been so angry.

How scaped I killing when I crossed you so? O insupportable and touching loss!

O Cassius, I am sick of many griefs. Portia is dead. Distressed by the killings in Rome and my absence, she fell **distract**, and swallowed fire.

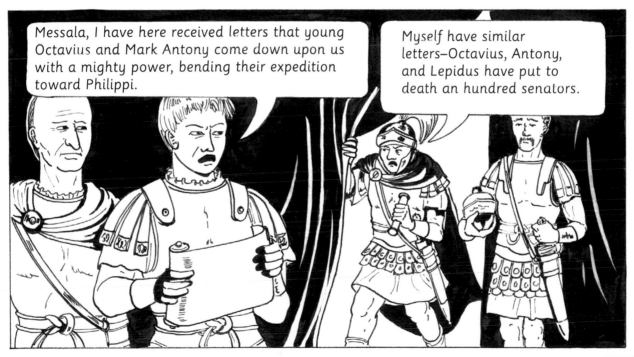

Messala, I have here received letters that young Octavius and Mark Antony come down upon us with a mighty power, bending their expedition toward Philippi.

Myself have similar letters–Octavius, Antony, and Lepidus have put to death an hundred senators.

distract— beside oneself, distraught

Act IV Scene iii	Brutus suggests that they march toward Philippi to meet the armies of Antony and Octavius. But Cassius is convinced that they should stay where they are and by the time the enemy reaches them, their armies will be worn out and easier to fight.

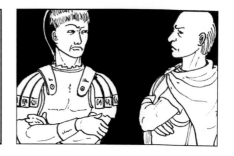

Brutus: Well, to our work **alive**. What do you think
Of marching to Philippi presently?

Cassius: I do not think it good.

Brutus: Your reason?

Cassius: This it is:
'Tis better that the enemy seek us;
So shall he waste his **means**, weary his soldiers,
Doing himself offense, whilst we, lying still,
Are full of rest, defense, and nimbleness.

Brutus: Good reasons must give place to better.
The people 'twixt Philippi and this ground
Do stand in a forced affection,
For they have grudged us contribution.
The enemy, marching along by them,
By then shall make a fuller number up,
Come on refreshed, new added, and encouraged,
From this advantage we shall cut him off
If at Philippi we do face him there,
And these people at our back.

alive—in life

means—resources

Think about it

Whose battle strategy or idea do you think is better? Brutus wants to attack immediately; and Cassius wants the enemy to wear themselves out and use up their resources, which will make them weak and easier to fight.

Cassius: Hear me, good brother.

Brutus: Under your pardon.
We have tried the utmost of our friends,
Our legions are full, our cause is ripe.
The enemy increaseth every day;
We, at the height, are ready to decline.
There is a tide in the affairs of men
Which, taken at the flood, leads on to fortune;
Omitted, all the voyage of their life
Is bound in shallows and in miseries.
On such a full sea are we now afloat,
And we must take the current when it serves
Or lose our ventures.

Cassius: Then, with your will, go on;
We'll along ourselves, and meet them at Philippi.

Brutus: The deep of night is crept upon our talk,
And nature must obey necessity,
There is no more to say.

Cassius: No more. Good night.
Early tomorrow will we rise and hence.

Literary terms
A sailing **metaphor** is used to compare the decisions that men make to the tides and currents of the sea.

Brutus calls Lucius, his servant, and a few soldiers into the tent to stay the night. He asks Lucius to play a song, but unable to sleep, Brutus sees the ghost of Caesar, who tells him that they will meet again at Philippi.

Lucius, where is thy instrument? Canst thou play thy instrument a strain or two?

Varro and Claudius lie in my tent and sleep. It may be I shall raise you on business to my brother Cassius.

Ay, my lord, it is my duty, sir.

So please you, sir.

Ha! who comes here? I think it is the weakness of mine eyes that shapes this monstrous **apparition**. Art thou anything?

Why com'st thou?

Why, I will see thee at Philippi then. Now I have taken heart thou vanishest, ill spirit, I would hold more talk with thee.

Thy evil spirit, Brutus.

To tell thee thou shalt see me at Philippi.

Literary terms
The use of **foreshadowing**, with the vision of the ghost of Caesar, foretells coming action.

apparition—ghost

44

| Act V Scene i | Octavius and Antony are on the battlefield with their armies when a messenger arrives to say that the enemy is approaching. The four generals meet, insult each other, and depart to prepare for battle. |

Villains! When your vile daggers hacked one another in the sides of Caesar, you **showed your teeth** like apes and fawned like hounds.

Prepare you, generals. The enemy comes on in gallant show. Their bloody sign of battle is hung out.

Defiance, traitors, hurl we in your teeth.

Caesar, thou canst not die by traitors' hands unless thou bring'st them with thee.

A **peevish schoolboy**, worthless of such honor, joined with a **masker and a reveler**!

showed your teeth—grinned
peevish schoolboy—i.e., Octavius
masker and a reveler—i.e., Antony

45

**Act V
Scene i**

Cassius confesses that it is his birthday and that he has changed his earlier disbelief in the meaning of omens.

Cassius: Messala, This is my birthday; as this very day
Was Cassius born. Give me thy hand, Messala.
Be thou my witness that against my will
(As Pompey was) am I compelled to set
Upon one battle all our liberties.
You know that I held **Epicurus** strong
And his opinion. Now I change my mind
And partly credit things that do **presage**
Coming from Sardis, on our former ensign
Two mighty eagles fell; and there they perched,
Gorging and feeding from our soldier's hands,
Who to Philippi here consorted us.
This morning they are fled away and gone,
And in their steads do **ravens, crows, and kites**
Fly o'er our heads and downward look on us
As we were sickly prey. Their shadows seem
A canopy most fatal, under which
Our army lies, ready to give up the ghost.

Messala: Believe not so.

Cassius: I but believe it partly,
For I am fresh of spirit and resolved
To meet all perils very constantly.

Epicurus—a Greek philosopher who denied the value of omens

presage—foretell

ravens, crows, and kites—birds that are associated with death

---

Literary terms

The use of an **allusion** in referring to a Greek philosopher's belief that omens were *not* predictors of future happenings demonstrates Cassius' change of feelings. Shakespeare in fact uses these omens (the appearance of ravens, crows, and kites) to **foreshadow** the deaths of the two conspirators.

Brutus and Cassius briefly discuss the possibilities in the forthcoming battles. Either they will live the rest of their days in peace, or they may never see each other alive again.

Cassius: Now, most noble Brutus,
The gods today stand friendly, that we may,
Lovers in peace, lead on our days to age!
But since the affairs of men rests still uncertain,
Let's reason with the worst that may befall.
If we do lose this battle, then is this
The very last time we shall speak together.
What are you then determinèd to do?

Brutus: Even by the rule of that philosophy
By which I did blame Cato for the death
Which he did give himself (I know not how,
But I do find it cowardly and vile,
For fear of what might fall, so to prevent
The time of life); arming myself with patience
To **stay the providence** of some high powers
That govern us below.

Cassius: Then, if we lose this battle,
You are contented to be led in triumph
Through the streets of Rome?

Brutus: No, Cassius, no. Think not, thou noble Roman,
That ever Brutus will go bound to Rome.
He bears too great a mind. But this same day
Must end that work the ides of March begun.
And whether we shall meet again, I know not.
Therefore our everlasting farewell take.
Forever and forever farewell, Cassius!
If we do meet again, why we shall smile;
If not, why then this parting was well made.

Cassius: Forever and forever farewell, Brutus!
If we do meet again, we'll smile indeed;
If not, 'tis true this parting was well made.

Brutus: Why then, lead on. —O, that a man might know
The end of this day's business ere it come!
But it sufficeth that the day will end,
And then the end is known. Come, ho! Away!

> **Think about it**
>
> What would it be like to say good-bye to a friend, not knowing whether you would ever see him/her again?

stay the providence—to await judgment

| Act V Scene ii | Antony's army battles with Cassius' men, and Octavius' army fights with Brutus' men. Brutus sends Messala with orders for Cassius' army, telling them to come down from the hills because Octavius' men lack the energy to fight. |

Ride, Messala, ride, and give these **bills** unto the legions on the other side. Let them set on at once; I perceive but a **cold demeanor** in Octavius' wing, and sudden push gives them the overthrow. Ride, let them all come down.

bills—orders, written messages
cold demeanor—a lack of fighting spirit

<table>
<tr><td>**Act V Scene iii**</td><td>Cassius sends Titinius up to his camp to see whether the men storming it are friends or enemies. Pindarus, who is observing the ruckus, mistakenly describes the scene to Cassius, with details of Titinius being captured. Cassius then commands Pindarus to stab him with the sword that he used to help kill Caesar.</td></tr>
</table>

O look, Titinius, look! The villains fly! Are those my tents where I perceive the fire? Mount my horse till he have brought thee up to yonder troops and back, that I may rest assured whether yond troops are friend or enemy.

I will be here again even with a thought.

Cassius: Go, Pindarus, get higher on that hill.
My sight was ever **thick**. Regard Titinius,
And tell me what thou not'st about the field.
This day I **breathèd first**. Time is come round,
And where I did begin, there shall I end.
My life is **run his compass**. Sirrah, what news?

Pindarus: Titinius is enclosed round about
With horsemen that make to him on the spur.
Yet he spurs on. Now they are almost on him.
Now Titinius! Now some light. O, he lights too!
He's Ta'en. And Hark! They shout for joy.

Cassius: Come down; behold no more.
O, coward that I am to live so long
To see my best friend ta'en before my face!
Come hither, sirrah.
In Parthia did I take thee prisoner,
And then I swore thee, saving of thy life,
That whatsoever I did bid thee do
Thou shouldst attempt it. Come now, keep thine oath.
Now be a freeman, and with this good sword,
That ran through Caesar's bowels, search this bosom.
Stand not to answer. Here, take thou the hilts,
And, when my face is covered, as 'tis now,
Guide thou the sword. Caesar thou art revenged
Even with the sword that killed thee. [*Cassius dies*]

thick—not clear, blurry

breathèd first—Cassius' birthday

run his compass—has come full circle

> **Think about it**
>
> Imagine having to keep a promise to someone that meant taking his life. Could you go through with it? Would you try to talk him out of it? How would you handle a situation like this?

Pindarus: So, I am free, yet would not so have been,
Durst I have done my will.—O Cassius!—
Far from this country Pindarus shall run,
Where never Roman shall take note of him. [*He exits*]

[*Enter Titinus and Messala*]

Messala: Where did you leave him?

Titinius: All disconsolate,
with Pindarus his bondman, on this hill.

Messala: Is not that he that lies upon the ground?

Titinius: No, this was he Messala,
But Cassius is no more. O setting sun
As in thy red rays thou dost sink to night,
So in his red blood Cassius' day is set!
The sun of Rome is set. Our day is gone;
Clouds, dews, and dangers come; our deeds are done.
Mistrust of my success hath done this deed.

Messala: Mistrust of good success hath done this deed.
O hateful Error, **melancholy's child**,
Why dost thou show to the apt thoughts of men
The things that are not?

Titinius: What, Pindarus! Where are thou, Pindarus?

Messala: Seek him, Titinius whilst I go to meet
The noble Brutus, thrusting this report
Into his ears. I may say "thrusting it,"
For piercing steel and **darts envenomed**
Shall be as welcome to the ears of Brutus
As tidings of this sight. [*Messala leaves*]

> **Literary terms**
> "… dews, and dangers come; our deeds are done" is an example of alliteration.

melancholy's child—sad people fear unreal dangers

darts envenomed—poisoned darts

Messala and Titinius return to find Cassius dead. Messala leaves to find Brutus. And Titinius, despondent over Cassius' death, stabs himself. Brutus finds both men dead and orders Cassius' body sent to Thasos.

Titinius: Why didst thou send me forth, brave Cassius?
Did I not meet thy friends, and did not they
Put on my brows this wreath of victory
And bid me give it thee? Didst thou not hear their shouts?
Alas, thou has misconstrued everything!
But hold thee, take this garland on thy brow.
Thy Brutus bid me give it thee, and I
Will do his bidding.—Brutus, come apace,
And see how I regarded Caius Cassius.—
By your leave, gods, this is a Roman's part.
Come, Cassius's sword, and find Titinius' heart. [*Stabs himself and dies*]
[*Brutus arrives with Messala, Young Cato, Strato, Volumnius and Lucilius*]

Brutus: Are yet two Romans living such as these?—
Friends, I owe more tears
To this dead man than you shall see me pay.
Come therefore, and to **Thasos** send his body.

Thasos—an island near Philippi

His funerals shall not be in our camp,
Lest it discomfort us.—Lucillius, come.—
And come, young Cato. Let us to the field.—
Labeo and Flavius, set our battles on.
'Tis three o'clock, and, Romans, yet ere night
We shall try fortune in a second fight.
                                   [*They exit*]

In the final battle of the war, Brutus, Messala, Young Cato, Lucilius, and Flavius are together. Brutus, Messala, and Flavius leave. Antony's soldiers arrive fighting. Cato is killed, but Lucilius pretends to be Brutus and is captured.

Antony: Where is he?

Lucilius: Safe, Antony, Brutus is safe enough.
I dare assure thee that no enemy
Shall ever take alive the noble Brutus.
The gods defend him from so great a shame!
When you do find him, or alive or dead,
He will be found like Brutus, like himself.

Antony: This is not Brutus, friend; but, I assure you,
A prize no less in worth. Keep this man safe.
Give him all kindness. I had rather have
Such men my friends than enemies. Go on,
And see whe'er Brutus be alive or dead,
And bring us word unto Octavius' tent
How everything is chanced.

Think about it

Have you ever taken the blame for something to prevent a friend from getting in trouble? Lucilius is rewarded for this act of courage. Is it truly a courageous act in this instance?

52

Act V
Scene v

Resting with his soldiers, Brutus asks Clitus, Dardanius, and then Volumnius to hold his sword so that he may run into it and kill himself, but they refuse, and leave when they see Antony's army approach. Left only with Strato, Strato holds the sword, and Brutus runs into it and dies. Antony and Octavius arrive and praise Brutus' good qualities, and the play is ended.

office—the service of   smatch—a touch of, or taste of

Also available in this series:

Twelfth Night
Twelfth Night – Teacher's Resource Book

Romeo and Juliet
Romeo and Juliet – Teacher's Resource Book

A Midsummer's Night Dream
A Midsummer's Night Dream – Teacher's Resource Book

Macbeth
Macbeth – Teacher's Resource Book